MOVING FORWARD
A NOVELLA OF LIFE AFTER ZOMBIES

JAMIE LACKEY

Dedication

For Paul

ACKNOWLEDGMENTS

Paul Stefko

Jenn Scott

Karen Birkedahl Rylander

Kathryn Jones

Barbara Carlson

Savannah Bozonier

Chris Aumiller

Frankie "Turnip Eyes" Oreto

Jeremy Zimmerman

Lois

Betsy Scarbro

Larry Ivkovich

Linda M McNair

Nathan Dziadul

Patrick J Ropp

A. B Treadwell

Justin Bolger

Kathryn Board

Tracey Levino

Vincent Baverso

Karen Strouss

Alison Wilgus

Mike Brendan

Amanda Lawson

Erik Graybill

Bill Moran

Pete Butler-Davis

Ailish Brundage

Richard Zapp

Elizabeth Mathers-Meeks

Malina Bowen

Ross Justin Pollock

Dan Hall

Victoria Boardley

Arthur McMahon

Laine Wooliscroft

Cory Livingston

Isaac 'Will It Work' Dansicker

Don and Debbie Lackey

Moving Forward

Butterflies flitted from flower to flower, and the summer air was heavy with laughter and the smell of fresh-cut grass. Corinne wiped orange baby food off of her granddaughter Melody's dark brown cheek, then spotted a lone zombie shambling out of the thick trees at the far end of the park. All around, young families continued their picnics.

The realization that even the parents were under thirty—that they were soft city children and none of them had ever seen a zombie with their own eyes—hit her, distant and horrible.

Instinct took over, and Corinne jumped to her feet, her knees protesting. The zombie spotted the closest family and broke into a shambling jog.

"What's up, Mom?" Kendall, her oldest daughter, said from the ground. Her face was as wide and innocent as the baby she cradled to her chest. Did she really not see it?

Corrine grabbed the bottle of wine and sprinted toward the zombie. "Run!" she shouted. "All of you, get out of here!"

It has been a long time she she'd been a decoy, and there was no sniper here, waiting to take the monster down. But her aim was still true. The bottle thunked into the zombie's shoulder, and it turned from its original prey.

The picnickers finally scattered, gathering their little ones and fleeing. At least they all knew not to scream.

The zombie moved toward her, and she backed off in bursts. There had to be forces on their way. All she had to do was keep it distracted and keep away from it.

Just like old times. Except her breath was already ragged and her legs ached—but she should still be a match for this single normal zombie.

Then a baby wailed, and the zombie's head turned. The family was standing on their picnic blanket, stuffing plastic plates into a basket. "Shit," Corinne hissed. The zombie started toward them.

"Run!" Corrine screamed.

The family froze, still clutching their plates.

Corinne charged and took the zombie down with a hard tackle. She hit the ground, let the zombie go, and rolled away. But she didn't get far enough. The zombie lunged at her. She managed to grab its shoulders and keep its snapping teeth away from her face. It stank of rotting flesh, and its strong arms were cool through its tattered clothes. It snarled and raked its fingernails through her hair, then bit deep into her forearm.

Gunshots rang out, and it slumped on top of her. A soldier ran up, incongruous in his gray camo body armor. "That was a brave thing you did, ma'am. Are you okay?"

Corinne shook her head. "I'm bit."

The soldier gave her a hand to her feet. "That's a damn shame."

She was already dizzy and cold. "My family—"

"No one else was injured, ma'am. They're fine. Let's get you to a clinic."

"Thanks," Corinne said. Her tongue was numb and swollen. Then strong arms wrapped around her, and darkness took her.

• • •

Corinne's whole body ached. She shifted, and padded cuffs pulled at her wrists and ankles. She forced her eyes open, and the bright fluorescent white of the hospital room stung. Two men and a woman with heavy black pistols stood at the foot of her bed. All three guns were pointed at her head.

The man on the left flipped his safety on and holstered his gun. "She's through it," he said, his gray eyes as cold as closed steel doors.

The chubby man on the right bent to unfasten the straps on her ankles, and the woman who'd stood in the center moved to her wrists. "How're you feeling?" she asked.

"Terrible."

The woman gave her a wry smile. "That'll pass. Welcome to the ranks of the infected."

Corinne spotted the black Z tattoos on the inside of each of their wrists, and saw them on her own when the woman freed her hands. She rubbed her wrists—the skin was smooth and even, already healed. The tattoos were harder to see on her darker skin, but still clear enough.

The bite on her arm had been dressed, and there was another

2

bandage over her abdomen. She touched it, and pain spiked through her.

"Careful," the chubby man said. "You don't want to pop your stitches."

"Stitches?" Corinne asked.

"From your hysterectomy. They don't want anyone getting pregnant in here, and it's safest to do any surgery while you're still changing."

Corinne laid a hand over the bandage and tried to feel the hollow where her womb had been. It just felt sore. She was too old to have more kids, anyway.

"Her family is waiting," the first man said from his position in the corner.

"How long was I out?" Corinne asked.

"About two weeks," the woman said.

The chubby man flipped through a chart. "16 days, to be precise. Would you like a hand sitting up?"

"That won't pop any stitches, will it?" Corinne asked.

He shook his head and helped her up. "I'm Carl, by the way. I'm one of the doctors, here."

"Where is here, exactly?" Corinne asked, even though she had a pretty solid suspicion.

"The South Bay Infected Sanctuary," the man in the corner said, his voice as cold as his eyes. "Where else?"

The woman rolled her eyes. "Don't mind Thomas, he just hates being on the welcoming committee. I'm Janet. I run this facility."

"Nice to meet you. I'm Corinne."

"We know," Thomas said. "Now, let's get her wheeled down to the visitation room before the daughter starts complaining that we're holding her away from her family against her will again."

Corinne sighed. That sounded like her younger daughter, Tara. "If she's on a rampage, we'd better get there as quick as we can."

Carl and Janet helped her into a wheelchair while Thomas stood with his hand resting on his gun. "If the meet and greet doesn't take too long, we can get your orientation started," he said.

Carl pushed her toward an elevator at the end of the hall, and Corinne wondered what she could possibly say to her family.

The observation room was split right down the center by a two-inch thick Plexiglas wall. The only opening was a hand-sized hole, right in the middle. Her family—her husband and two daughters—stood clustered on the other side. Darnell looked like he'd been sleeping in his jeans and wrinkled flannel shirt. Kendall mirrored him, also in jeans with her long braids in a tangled mess. Tara, in her pinstriped pantsuit and fresh makeup, looked like she belonged in a different family.

Her throat ached when she saw them, but she pushed that away. Her pain was for later. When she was alone.

"Mom!" Tara shouted. She pressed both palms against the glass. "Are you okay?"

Corinne bit her lip to keep from snapping at the stupid question. "Yeah," she lied. "I'm just fine."

"Are they treating you okay?"

"I just woke up, but everyone seems nice enough."

"Good. The governor assures me that this is the very best sanctuary in the state."

Kendall came up to the glass next to her sister. "It's a relief to see you alive," she said, her cheeks wet. "We were really worried."

"It's good to see you, too. How are you? How's Melody?"

"We're okay. And Melody's good. Home with her father. How are you feeling?" Kendall asked.

"Overwhelmed," Corinne said. That sounded like an acceptable answer. She forced a small smile. "But glad to be alive."

Darnell barked a laugh as he joined their daughters at the glass wall. "Girls, can I have a minute with your mother?"

"Sure thing, Daddy," Kendall said. She took Tara's arm and pulled her away. The door clicked behind them.

"What the hell were you thinking?" Darnell asked. He looked old and tired in the harsh light.

"I was thinking that I was in a park full of children, and someone had to stop the zombie."

"That someone didn't have to be you. It's not your job to protect everyone, Corinne. There were soldiers coming."

"Are you really saying that I should have just stood by?"

"Yes. That is exactly what you should have done. Instead, you had to play the hero and get yourself killed."

"I'm not dead," Corinne snapped. Her chest felt tight.

"No? What's that on your wrist, then?"

Corinne couldn't talk, couldn't move. What hell was happening to her? Her heart thundered in her ears, and the world went gray. Her whole body shuddered.

Cool, dry hands wrapped around hers. "Breathe, Corinne. Breathe. Remember who you are. Count to ten."

The sound of her heartbeat faded. Corinne slumped in her wheelchair and looked up into Thomas's eyes. This time, the cold gray was a comfort. "What just happened?" she asked.

Thomas squeezed her hands again. "I'll explain during orientation. Right now, I want you to look up at the camera and wave." He turned to Darnell. "I think you should leave."

Corinne saw unveiled disgust on her husband's face and flinched. She looked away and waved at the camera. The doors and the tiny opening in the glass hissed open—they must have closed when she'd been...indisposed.

"Yeah," Darnell said. "Leaving is probably for the best."

When he was gone, Thomas gave her a level look. "Nice guy."

"He's upset," Corinne said, feeling defensive and shaken.

Thomas shrugged. "The other new girl has a visitor, too. I have to stay to keep an eye on things. Do you want to wait here, too?"

Corinne shrugged. "I don't have anywhere else to be."

Thomas waved at the camera in the corner of the room. A moment later, a girl came in. She'd taken the time to put on some makeup and normal clothes. She was pretty, in a wholesome, outdoorsy way. Her Z tattoos looked out of place. She walked up to the wall and took a deep breath.

The door on the other side opened, and a young man came in. His eyes were bloodshot, and it looked like it had been days since he'd slept or shaved. He went straight to the hole in the glass that Corinne's family had ignored and shoved his arm as far through as it would go.

"What are you doing, Danny?" the girl asked.

"Quick, Nancy, you have to bite me."

Nancy took a step back. "Danny, stop it," she hissed. She glanced over at Corinne and Thomas. Thomas's hand rested on his pistol. Corinne tried to look as bored and cool as he did. She figured she succeeded as well as she could in her hospital gown.

"It's the only way we can be together."

"You could die. And if you survive, I could turn any second. Or you could turn any second. It's not romantic. Get your damn arm out of that hole."

"Please, Nancy."

She shook her head and pulled a ring off of her right ring finger. She held it for a second, then dropped it into his palm. A tiny diamond glinted in his palm. "Don't come back, Danny. Find someone else. Be happy."

"Nancy, please!"

Nancy turned away. Tears glistened on her cheeks. "Goodbye, Danny."

"You heard the lady," Thomas said. "Are you going to go, or is security going to remove you?"

Danny glared at him. "Fuck you, zombie."

"You're not my type, son. Get out."

Danny stared at Nancy for another long moment, then pulled his arm back. "I love you, and this is yours. Even if you don't want it anymore." He laid the ring on the narrow ledge. "I—I'm sorry. I—just don't know what I'll do without you. I love you. I hope you do manage to be happy, here. You—you know how to reach me when you want to talk."

When he left, Nancy walked over and took the ring back. She stared at it, then put in in the pocket of her jeans. She scrubbed tears away with the back of her hand.

"I'll go find us a classroom," Thomas said. "You two introduce yourselves while I'm gone. And Corinne, get out of that idiotic chair, you don't need it."

Corrine locked the wheels and stood carefully. The pain in her abdomen was almost gone. She turned to Nancy. "Hey, you okay?" she asked.

Nancy's eyes filled, and she shook her head.

Corinne's maternal instincts took over—she held out her arms, and the girl fell into them. Hot tears soaked into her hospital gown. "I'm sorry" she sobbed.

"Shh, it's okay. You're allowed to cry." She rubbed Nancy's back and patted her blonde head. Thomas poked his head into the room to collect them, and Corinne gave him a hard glare. He held his hands up and mouthed, "I'll wait right here."

After a while, Nancy's sobs eased. "Thanks," she said, blushing. "I just—"

"I understand."

Nancy looked down at her wrists. "I guess you do."

"You ready to start our orientation?"

Nancy nodded. "You know what the worst part was?"

"What?"

"When Danny stuck his arm in here and starting waving it around, it was like—like I could smell it. And it smelled delicious."

Corinne stifled a shudder.

"I hope it was just my imagination," Nancy said. "But I don't think it was."

• • •

Thomas led them to a small, sunny room. Corinne and Nancy sat side-by-side on a plush couch. The large windows looked out onto a well-maintained garden. Outside, flowers sagged in the sun. A woman in a baseball cap and thick gloves wandered around with a hose.

"Rule one," Thomas said, holding up a single finger, "is to never, ever fake an episode." He switched on a flat screen TV, and security footage played. A woman walked along a hallway, then she stopped, her shoulders hunched in, and her hands went to her temples. Her whole body shook, and she gasped for breath. Then her arms relaxed. She looked up and hissed.

Thomas paused it. "You will see episodes. You'll have them yourselves. Corinne, you had one already."

Corinne nodded, remembering the feeling of her body closing in around her.

"They happen if you get sick or scared or stressed. Sometimes they happen for no discernible reason at all. But the hiss—" he rewound it and played the last few seconds again, "that's the point of no return."

He held up a second finger. "Rule two is to carry your firearm at all times. If any of us turns, it is the others' responsibility to put the monster down. Aim for the head. There is no overkill. To destroy the creatures we become, the entire brain has to be destroyed. Once a monster is down, you empty your clip in its skull. Then take the gun off its body and empty that, too."

He ticked up a third finger. "Firearm proficiency is not optional. You will train up to an acceptable level, and then you will maintain that level. There will be periodic tests. You will pass them. If not, you will retrain."

"What if we refuse?" Nancy asked. "Not that I'm refusing. I'm just—just curious."

Thomas sighed. "We're not slaves here, and no one is going to force you to do anything against your will. But if you refuse to follow the rules, you'll be a danger to others, and will be confined to your room."

He pointed to the security camera. "Get used to those. They are everywhere, and they are your friends."

"What exactly do you mean by 'everywhere'?" Corinne asked, glancing up at the camera's single gray eye.

"I mean everywhere. Every inch of this place has camera coverage. Privacy is no longer a luxury you have. The cameras are always on, and someone is always watching them. When an episode begins, they are responsible for locking the facility down. Lockdown doesn't end until the person suffering from the episode looks up at the camera and waves. Or till they're put down."

"What happens if they're alone? Or if they kill everyone else with them?" Corinne asked.

"Then we gas them. It doesn't kill them, but a high enough concentration stops them long enough for us to go in and get the job done."

Corinne noticed vents lining the floorboards and shuddered. The whole complex could be a death trap at the push of a button.

"Who watches the cameras?" Nancy asked.

"People volunteer for shifts."

"Creepy voyeur people," Nancy muttered.

Thomas arched an eyebrow. "Monitoring the cameras is an important job, and I expect both of you to take at least one rotation as you try out various positions within the complex."

"Positions? Like jobs?" Nancy asked.

"Yes. The government provides us with food, utilities, and shelter. You're expected to find some way to make yourself useful. There's lots to do—we can't bring in any outsiders, so we're expected to do everything from internal security to cooking to janitorial work ourselves."

That didn't sound unreasonable to Corinne—she'd been wondering how they were supposed to fill their days. Though going from an executive administrative assistant to a janitor hadn't exactly been her career plan.

It had been a long time since she'd had to rebuild her life—there'd been a time that she'd have scoffed at the futility of trying to plan at all.

"What do you do?" Nancy asked

"I'm the firearms instructor. And head of internal security."

Nancy sighed and looked out the window. "I was going to be a doctor."

"You still can," Thomas said. "We like to have multiple backups for important positions. We can arrange for you to continue your studies remotely."

Nancy perked up. "Really? Are you serious?"

Thomas nodded. "There's no need to put your life on hold."

Nancy barked a laugh. "My life is over." She touched the tan line on her bare finger, then rubbed the Z on her right wrist. "But it'll be nice to get a little bit of it back."

"Letting go of the past is good." Thomas said. "Your previous lives are over, that's certainly true. But you're not dead. And even though you're limited by the walls of this complex, there are still plenty of opportunities to lead a rich, meaningful life. Are you two ready for the tour?"

"Can I put on some real clothes first?" Corinne asked. "I know we're letting go of privacy, but I'd like pants."

"Of course, we'll make your rooms our first stop. Follow me."

• • •

Corinne's room was narrow and gray, but the window looked out over the garden. The high wall that surrounded the complex blocked out all but a sliver of the faded blue sky, but the garden itself was sunny, filled with rows of crops, patches of flowers, and even a few scattered stands of trees. She imagined zombies lurking in the shadows and turned away.

She found her clothes in the drawers built into the base of the bed and her laptop and purse on the desk. She dropped the hospital gown onto the dark gray carpet and kicked the disposable flip flop slippers they'd given to her into the corner.

She wriggled her toes in the rough, thin fiber. They'd just installed a new, super-plush carpet in her bedroom at home.

Her clothes still smelled like her fresh linen laundry detergent.

She sat down on the bed and buried her face in her hands. Her emotions felt too big for her body. She'd never hold her daughters again; never cradle her granddaughter against her chest.

Never have sex with her husband.

Her husband, who'd looked at her like a monster.

It was even worse than losing Aasha, worse than the night that the zombies had come to her hometown and killed everyone she'd ever known. At least then, there'd been something to move on to—a purpose that she could devote herself to. An enemy to fight.

She looked down at her wrists. She was essentially one of those enemies now. A monster waiting to happen.

"I just want to wake up," she whispered. But that wasn't an option. She stood up, put one foot in front of the other. Explored her room.

There was a tiny bathroom with a toilet, sink, and shower through a narrow door. Pale blue tiles lined the floor and walls, and a tiny glass block window let in thin light. Her toothbrush perched in a metal rack, and her various soaps were hung in a basket on the showerhead. She wondered which of her family members had packed her things. She doubted that it was Darnell. Maybe Kendall? Did she think of everything on her own, or did they give her a list?

She wanted her own bed and her own shower and her sunny kitchen and tiny deck. She wanted to be able to cry without anyone watching.

She shoved her legs into her favorite jeans. The pain in her stomach was completely gone, and she pulled the tape and gauze away to look at it.

The scar looked months—maybe years—old. She tore the dressing off of her forearm. She couldn't even see the bite-mark.

"What the hell am I?" she whispered.

Someone knocked on the door. "Are you decent?" Thomas asked.

"Hold on a sec." She grabbed a shirt at random and pulled it on.

He stood in the hallway, his gunmetal eyes cool and his face blank. "You ready for the rest of the tour?"

"Sure."

Nancy poked her head out of a doorway down the hall. "I'm getting a shower. I'll be quick." She slammed the door shut before Thomas could protest. Corinne waited for him to stalk down the hall and pound on the door, but he just sighed and leaned against the wall. "You can grab a shower, too, if you'd like."

Corinne shook her head. She imagined standing in the shower and crying and never being able to stop.

Poor Nancy—she wondered if she'd wanted children. At least Corinne had lived a good portion of a normal life. "What's your story?" Corinne asked, leaning next to Thomas. "How did you end up here?"

Thomas rubbed his Z tattoo. It was uneven at the edges, like it had been done in a hurry, and faded. "I was one of the very first people here. Before that, I worked as a scout for the military. I was bit when I was 13. I was youngest to ever survive. And now I've been infected longer than anyone else."

"How long is that?"

Thomas arched an eyebrow at her.

"No more privacy, remember? I'm 52, and I've been infected for about 16 days."

"I'm 48, and I've been infected for 35 years."

"You were bit in the first year of the war?"

"Yeah."

"How have you kept it together, all this time?"

He shrugged. "It's been close, a few times. When I woke up, right after, I found my sister eating my mother. She'd killed herself after we were bit—she'd never been big on confrontation. I almost lost it right there."

Corinne wondered if his mother had smelled like food, but didn't ask. "What's your secret?"

"I don't have one."

"I don't believe you."

"Maybe I've just been lucky."

"Lucky? To have lived like this for 35 years?"

"It's better than the alternative," he said.

"I suppose that's true. It's just hard to see it that way right now." She thought of her home again, and her throat tightened.

"The first few weeks are the worst. Things'll be better once you're

11

settled in."

Corinne studied his face.

A faint flush spread across his cheeks. "What?"

"You really care, don't you? The whole distant facade is an act. I bet you volunteered to be in charge of orientation. And I bet you really pour yourself into the security around this place, and I bet you're very serious about making sure that we all pass our firearms proficiency tests."

He crossed his arms over his chest. "What makes you say that?"

"You backed off when I was comforting Nancy. You didn't give her any crap about her shower, and you let me come here for pants."

"None of that means that I care about you."

"I never said you cared about me—I said you cared about all of us."

A smile tugged at the corners of his lips. He had a nice smile. "I feel sorry for your kids," he said. "I bet they had a hard time getting anything past you."

Corinne laughed. "They never even tried. If they had crap to pull, they'd take it to their father."

Nancy came back out. Her hair was wet and eyes were red. "Let's go."

"Our first stop is the cafeteria," Thomas said. "Are either of you hungry?"

Corinne nodded. "I could eat."

"Yeah, me too," Nancy said.

The cafeteria was a long, narrow room. "In case of lockdown, this is actually divided into six sections," Thomas said, pointing out the blast doors that would lower from the ceiling. "It's a good idea not to stand directly under them, just in case."

"Great," Nancy muttered. They each claimed a plastic tray.

"Our menu changes daily and we do our best to respect any and all dietary restrictions," Thomas said.

Corinne grabbed a piece of pizza, an apple, and a cardboard carton of chocolate milk. It was all decent, but not great.

"Can we have coffee?" Nancy asked, poking at her macaroni and cheese.

Thomas shook his head. "No caffeine, no alcohol."

"Do they increase the likelihood of an… incident?" Corinne asked.

Thomas shook his head. "Not really. The taxpayers just don't want to supply us with luxuries."

Nancy glared at her milk. "Coffee's not a luxury, it's a necessity."

Thomas shrugged. "Uncle Sam doesn't think so."

"Uncle Sam's a dick."

"No arguments here," Thomas said.

The tour continued through the four wings of living quarters, each with their own lounge area, the gym, the indoor obstacle course, the Olympic-sized pool, the kitchens, the gardens, the library, the security offices, the assorted distance-learning classrooms, and finally, the shooting range and attached armory.

"Let's get you each a sidearm and see what level you'll each be starting at."

The pistol was a cold, unfamiliar weight in Corrine's hand. She'd never had to shoot the zombies—her job had been to run.

Aasha had tried to teach her to shoot a sniper rifle. She took a deep breath and pushed the memory away.

Nancy took her gun and inspected it. "I suppose this will do." She took her place and emptied her clip into the target. Corinne took her own place and took her shots. They each at least hit the paper target, if not the black outline of a man.

Thomas examined each of their targets. "Nancy, great job. Corinne, you're going to need some serious work."

Corinne looked down at the gun. "Great."

• • •

Thomas drew them up a schedule for their first month, including shifts at each job in the compound. "I've scheduled in time for recreation and fitness training. I also highly recommend hand-to-hand combat training. Corinne, I'll be seeing you in the firing range tomorrow. Nancy, your proficiency test will be the next day, first thing in the morning. Before I go leave you, what are the two most important rules?"

"Never fake an episode and always carry our sidearm," Nancy said. She patted the gun on her hip. "I think we'll manage."

"Good. I'll leave you two to settle in, then."

"That's it? The whole orientation? A tour and two rules?"

Thomas nodded. "It's not a complicated place."

"Thank you for showing us around," Corinne said.

Thomas graced her with another smile. "It was my pleasure."

The gun at Corinne's hip was an unfamiliar bulge, and she kept bumping it with her arm as she and Nancy wandered down the hall toward their rooms.

"Well, at least I get voyeur duty out of the way first thing," Nancy said, eyeing her schedule.

Corinne examined her own schedule. "I start out in the library."

"Well, we don't have anywhere to be till tomorrow morning. Want to go a swim or something?"

"Can I take a rain check? I—I'd just like to be alone for a while."

"Yeah, I get it."

"Want to meet up for breakfast?"

Nancy smiled. "Yeah, that'll be nice. See you then."

Corinne went up to her room. She threw the holstered gun on the bed, then cried in the shower, and again under her covers. She missed Darnell's weight and warmth beside her.

Tara, her younger, politically-minded daughter, had used her influence to get them visas for a trip to Europe—the continent had been hit hard by the zombie plague, and travel restrictions were almost impossible to navigate, but Corrine had always wanted to see the Eiffel Tower, and Tara had been determined to make it happen. Their flight had been a week away when she'd tackled that zombie.

She buried her face in her pillow. Darnell was right—she was a fool.

And now she'd never see Paris. Never leave this gray building ever again. She glanced at the gun—it was a black shadow in the moonlight. She wondered how many newly infected people turned their guns on themselves during the first night.

It would be an easy way out. But the easy way out had never been something Corinne looked for.

She stared up at the ceiling as tears leaked down her cheeks and soaked into her hair. She hadn't cried herself to sleep for decades, and she couldn't face doing it tonight. She climbed out of bed, washed her face in cold water, belted the gun around her waist, and went to the library. She'd had stacks of books at home that she'd been meaning to read. Maybe she'd finally have time, now.

A part of her scoffed at the rest, scrambling for some silver lining to this disaster.

She reminded that voice that she'd managed to rise from the ashes from two lives already. "I can do this," she whispered to herself.

• • •

A few lamps burned in the library, but there was no one else around. She wandered through the stacks. Most of the books were old and worn—probably donated by other libraries that had been getting rid of them anyway. She ran her fingers along their plastic-coated spines.

She couldn't face anything heavy or serious. Eventually, she selected a romantic romp set in the Greek Isles, written long before the Zombie War. As she settled in to read it, the doors hissed closed. Steel shutters slid down over the windows. A minute passed, then two. Corinne tried to read, but her eyes kept flicking toward the sealed door.

How long did incidents last?

She stared at the same sentence, read the same words over and over.

It couldn't possibly be just an incident. Someone had turned. She comforted herself that probably wasn't anyone she'd met.

But what if it was? What if it was Nancy? Or Thomas? Her stomach twisted.

She heard booted footsteps running in the hallway. Another ten minutes dragged by. The door opened, and the shutters rolled back up.

She tried to read.

• • •

The next morning, Corinne looked around the cafeteria. Seeing everyone wearing side arms felt almost as strange as wearing one herself—handguns had been in limited supply during the war. The gun was an uncomfortable bulge on her belt. It caught on the edge of an empty table, and she stumbled. She couldn't imagine it ever feeling comfortable.

She spotted Nancy, and was surprised by the wave of relief she felt. The younger woman didn't look any better rested that Corinne felt. She'd finally been exhausted enough to sleep at 3AM, and her alarm had pinged insistently at 6.

They claimed a small table by the window. A few of the others gave welcoming smiles, the rest ignored them. Nancy poked at her dish of oatmeal. "If they really expect me to face 6AM on a regular basis without coffee, they have another thing coming."

"A cup of tea would be pretty welcome right now." Corinne tried the orange juice and grimaced. Darnell had planted an orange tree about a decade ago, and they hadn't bought bottled juice since.

"What did you do, before?" Nancy asked.

"I worked in an office. Setting up appointments and the like."

"Any family?"

Corinne nodded. "A husband, two daughters. A granddaughter. You?"

"Well, I had Danny. And my parents, two brothers, and a sister."

"Why didn't they come visit?"

Nancy scowled and rubbed her wrist. "They're against sheltering the infected. Think we should all just be shot. Safer that way. If Danny hadn't been there, they probably would have put me down." She ate a few bites of oatmeal. "I agreed with them. Just accepted that they were right without ever questioning it. And now here I am, set to leach off the taxpayers for the rest of my life. I always figured I'd kill myself if this ever happened, but I just can't. And I'm glad. I—I don't want to die, Corinne."

Corinne patted her hand. "Darnell—my husband—agrees with your parents. I agree with you. As long as we're alive, we have to keep going."

"I was thinking about it last night. About how any of us could turn at any time. It gave me nightmares. I've never really had nightmares before."

Corrine couldn't even remember a time without nightmares. "How did you get bit?"

"I brought Danny home to meet my folks. We met our freshman year of college, and just got engaged a couple of months ago. I couldn't put it off any longer. He was hurt that I didn't want to take him to meet them, and they were angry that I was going to marry some college boy. A liberal college boy, at that. My brothers insisted on taking him out shooting. My family runs a farm, out by the edge of zombie country. Anyway, they went shooting, and I went along. The zombie was in a ditch—it must've had its legs blown off in the minefield and dragged itself along through the grass. None of us saw it. My brothers were too busy harassing Danny and I was too busy glaring at them. Danny was the first to spot it. He shouted at me to look out, but it was too late. It got me in the calf. Next thing I knew, I was here. I don't even know how Danny got me out of there. It must have been horrible for him." She shuddered. "How about you?"

"I was at the park with my family. It all just happened so fast." Corinne felt a flash of guilt for holding back the details, but she didn't want to get into her history over breakfast. And Nancy was dealing with enough crap already.

"I'd better go get to my spying." Nancy rolled her eyes. "I'll be glad when it's done."

"Want to meet me in the library after? We can go for a walk and get dinner before I have to go to my shooting class."

"Make it a swim instead of a walk, and I'm in."

"Deal."

Nancy stood and picked up her tray. "Hey, Corinne?"

"Yeah?"

"Thanks. I mean, for being willing to listen—for being my friend. It's—it's helping."

"The feeling's mutual."

Last night, the library had started to feel like her personal sanctuary. This morning, it was full of bustling strangers, and the pages glared in the harsh morning sunlight. Corinne approached the desk in the middle of the large room. "I'm assigned to help out here today."

The middle-aged woman at the desk looked vaguely familiar. She wore heavy blue eye shadow and a long, sweeping black dress. Her graying hair cascaded around her face in soft ringlets. She sighed and rolled her eyes dark-lined eyes. "We just finished all the shelving. I guess you could get me some coffee."

"There isn't any coffee here."

The woman chuckled. "Cute. There isn't any coffee in the cafeteria. We are allowed to order things, you know."

"I didn't know that, actually."

"How like our Thomas, to leave that tidbit out. Anyway, there's a coffee pot in the backroom, just through that door. I take it black, with two sugars. You can go ahead and get yourself some, too."

The librarian definitely rubbed Corrine the wrong way, but she didn't want to start a fight. And coffee did sound nice. The break room was small and tidy, and the freshly-brewed coffee smelled heavenly. Corrine resolved to steal some for Nancy on the way out. She had a feeling that Nancy's family wouldn't be sending any care packages.

She poured herself a cup with lots of cream and stirred sugar into a mug for the librarian. She took it back out, and tried out her warmest smile. "Here you go."

"Thanks."

"I'm Corrine, by the way."

"I know, your name is on the schedule."

"What's your name?" Corrine struggled to keep her tone friendly.

"Oh, you don't recognize me?"

Corrine didn't like her coy tone any better than she'd liked her backhanded orders. "I do feel like I've seen you before, but I can't place you."

"I suppose not everyone reads. I'm Eliana Kirsch."

"Oh." Corrine supposed that it made sense for the famous infected author to work in the library. She'd never read any of her stuff—it had always sounded too depressing.

Eliana laughed. "At least you've heard of me."

"Yeah."

"Well, why don't you wander around and familiarize yourself with the layout. I'm actually in the middle of something, so I can't really give you a tour. Eric should be here in an hour or so, you can ask him if you have any questions."

Corrine had already wandered around the library last night, so she understood the general layout. She wandered idly into fiction, sipping her coffee. It was very good coffee.

There was a whole shelf devoted to Eliana's novels. She pulled one down and read the back—it was a story about the war, and about the lives it had ruined. Depressing.

The back flap contained a picture of a (much younger) Eliana, sundrenched and laughing on the deck of a sailboat. She'd been raised in money, and then lost her whole family to the zombies. Corrine sipped her coffee again and noted that it didn't say anything about losing her money.

Corrine wondered what happened to all of her own worldly

possessions. Her name was on the deed to their house. She had a savings account in her own name. There were three rows of computers by the windows, so she did a quick search on the infecteds' rights.

Apparently, inmates in infected shelters were still allowed to do outside work, if it could be performed remotely. A portion of their earnings went to the shelter, but they were free to do as they wished with the rest. She should still be able to access her own money—she didn't have any trouble logging onto her bank's website and checking the balance, anyway.

Her job wasn't one of the things that she'd miss. She didn't even have any coworkers that she'd been close to.

An older man tapped her on the shoulder. "Are you Corinne?"

"Yes. Are you Eric?"

He nodded. "You can stay and browse the internet if you want, but I do have some clerical things that I could use your help with."

Corinne smiled at him. "I'd love to help."

• • •

The day passed quickly. Eric was quiet and easy to work with. Eliana sat at the main desk and typed all day.

"If she's just going to write, why pretend to be helping?" Corinne asked.

Eric shrugged. "She's sure it adds to her mystique. She grew up in the lap of luxury, and now she's the librarian at an infected shelter."

"Have you ever read her stuff?"

"Yeah. It's really good. And she knows it."

Corinne was surprised. She'd imagined that it was overwrought drivel. "Well, at least she's got the talent to back up her attitude."

Eric snorted. "I'm not sure any amount of talent could back up her attitude."

At the end of her shift, Corinne grabbed a Styrofoam mug and filled it with coffee. She had no idea how Nancy took it, so she snagged a couple of sugars and a plastic cup of creamer, too. She hid it behind her body as she walked past Eliana, who didn't even glance up from her laptop.

Nancy was already waiting outside the door. "Hey, I saw that your boss has coffee, somehow."

Corinne had forgotten that Nancy was watching all day. She

fought back a shudder as she handed Nancy the cup.

"Oh my gosh, you're an angel."

"Apparently, we can buy stuff and have it shipped here."

"That explains a lot. There are people with tons of things stashed in their rooms. All I've got is one set of my own clothes and some random hand-me-downs that only kinda fit. She plucked at the overlarge t-shirt that she wore over same pair of jeans that she'd been wearing yesterday. "I don't really want to think about where they came from, you know?"

"Yeah."

"How was your day? Your boss looks like a real treat."

"She's a famous author, and didn't like that I didn't recognize her."

"Ooof."

"Yeah. Do you want to go grab our swimsuits?"

Nancy shook her head. "I don't have one. And since there's no privacy here anyway, I figured I'd just skinny dip. But we can run up if you want to grab your suit."

"No, I can do without, too. Solidarity and all that. How was voyeur duty?"

"Not as bad as I thought. I was in Watch Station A. Apparently there are three separate stations, just in case someone working has an incident. There's not a lot of judging going on. They're really serious about watching for incidents. We saw one, but he pulled through and waved and it was fine. There were a couple of tense moments there, though. It really drives the point home, you know? That we're all dangerous, no matter how normal we seem on the surface."

Corinne hadn't even noticed, but the library must have locked down during the incident. She wondered if it was good or bad that she was so quick to get used to that element of her new life.

The pool was empty when they arrived, with no visible lifeguard on duty. Just the ever present camera coverage. They piled their clothes in a corner. Corrine ran her fingers over the faded scar on her belly—Nancy's was almost gone, too.

"I haven't been skinny dipping in a long time," Nancy said.

"Me neither." There had been a swimming hole in the tiny town where she grew up. She wondered if it was still there.

She knew that the town wasn't.

Soft classical music played overhead, from speakers mounted in the corners. The ceiling was glass, the walls pretty pale green tile, and the sun was pleasantly hot against Corinne's bare skin. She wasn't a strong swimmer, but the water felt lovely as she paddled around.

"Do you mind if I do some laps?" Nancy asked.

Corinne shook her head. "I'm just going to float here."

The water buoyed her, and the music flowed around her. Mozart, followed by Brahms. She'd taken the girls to the symphony every year when they were in high school. Kendall had loved it. Tara, not so much.

The symphony was another thing that she'd never do again.

Nancy finished her laps and splashed over, her face flushed and her breath ragged. "I got called in to talk with Janet at lunchtime. She's arranged some distance-learning classes for me to continue my medical training."

"I think I met her—she was one of the people pointing a gun at my head when I woke up."

"Yeah, me too. She's apparently in charge. She seems nice."

The door opened, and Thomas strode in, wearing black swim trunks. "Speaking of things that seem nice," Nancy whispered. She waggled her eyebrows, and Corinne giggled.

He did have nice shoulders and incredible abs. He glanced at them and actually blushed. "Why are you two naked?"

"Nancy doesn't have a swimsuit."

"Plus, privacy is a thing of the past, remember?" Nancy said.

"Privacy yes, modesty, no."

"We can go if it makes you uncomfortable," Corinne started up the steps, and Thomas turned away, now bright red down to his chest. A moment later, he dove into the water and started swimming laps.

They got dressed and ventured back outside in silence.

"He was totally checking you out from the corner of his eye," Nancy said.

Corinne scoffed. "If he's checking anyone out, it's you, Miss Perky-tits."

Nancy laughed. "I'm pretty sure that's my new favorite nickname. I'm also pretty sure it was you he was looking at."

Speculating about Thomas made the ache in her heart fade a bit, even though it did make her feel a bit guilty. "Well, he's certainly not hard to look at, himself."

"I never would have guessed he was shy."

"Me neither."

They made their way to the cafeteria, and Corinne made herself a salad, while Nancy grabbed a couple slices of pizza. The salad smelled a bit odd—Corinne had never noticed lettuce having a smell before—but it tasted normal.

"So, do you think my debit card would still work?" Nancy asked. "I'm pretty sure I saw my wallet in a drawer in my room, and I have a bit of money saved up." Her shoulder sagged a bit. "It was supposed to be for the honeymoon."

"Well, then you should definitely spend on things that will make you happy."

Nancy tried to smile, and almost succeeded. "What do you miss most?"

"Darnell squeezed me fresh orange juice every morning. While I was showering, he'd go out and pick oranges. Then he'd bring me a tall glass of juice, and he'd smell like oranges and sunshine and him."

"So, you two had a good marriage?"

Corinne winced at the past tense. "Yeah." She remembered the look on his face after her incident, and frowned down at her salad.

"I'm sorry."

Corinne shrugged. "It is what it is. I loved him, and he loved me, and we can't be together anymore. Like you and Danny."

"Do you think it will get easier?"

She remembered Aasha's face. Then she thought of Thomas's abs. "I'm sure it will. It always does."

• • •

"You don't have to come to the range with me," Corinne said.

Nancy shrugged. "I know, but I like shooting. And maybe I can help."

They donned their protective ear-and eye-wear and started practicing.

"You lived through the war, right?" Nancy asked between shots.

Corinne nodded.

"How'd you manage to not learn to shoot?"

"I was a runner. I didn't have to shoot anything."

"Wait. You mean you were one of those crazy kids that acted as bait?"

"Yeah."

"And you didn't even have a gun? What if you ran into someone like us—a survivor who turned—a living zombie?"

Corinne shrugged. "I trusted my sniper. She had my back. And I was pretty fast, back then."

"Jesus. I'd never trust someone else to shoot the zombies while I ran away."

"Maybe you would have been a better sniper."

Nancy looked at Corinne's target. "It looks like a good thing that you weren't. Here, let me watch you take a couple of shots."

Corinne held the gun steady in both hands, aimed, and fired.

"Okay, your grip looks good, but you need to squeeze the trigger, not jerk it."

Corinne gave her a look, but tried to obey.

"Okay, that's a bit better. I think you're anticipating the recoil, though. Try not to brace for it before it happens—it'll throw off your aim."

"Right," Corinne muttered.

When the mandated 45 minute session was up, Corinne had only made a tiny amount of progress.

"Don't get discouraged—you are getting better!"

Corinne sighed. "Thanks. And thanks for the tips, they did help."

"Anytime. Want to come the library and help me pick what kind of coffee machine I should order?"

"Why don't you come to my room and use my laptop?"

"Your room came with a laptop?"

"It was mine, from before. My family must have dropped it off."

"I wonder if Danny would get me some things from my dorm room. I hate to ask him, though. After.. well, you know."

"He still loves you. I'm sure he'd be happy to help. And maybe when he's calmer, the two of you can get some closure." She thought about Darnell. Had she really only been here—awake, anyway—for one full day? It felt so much longer.

A somber-looking young man intercepted them at the staircase to their rooms. "Ms. Jackson? The supervisor needs to see you in her office."

"It's almost 10PM," Corinne said.

"I know, ma'am. And I'm sorry, but something's come up. Please come with me."

"I'll just go to my room," Nancy said. "Come get me, after, okay?"

Corinne followed the young man down the hall. He was dressed in an official-looking uniform, with a name-patch on his chest that said Riley.

"Is Riley your first or last name?" Corinne asked.

He gave her an uncomfortable grin. "Neither, ma'am. It's a hand-me-down uniform, just happened to fit. My name is Devon."

"How long have you been here, Devon?"

"About six months."

"Can you give me any idea of what's going on?"

He shook his head. "Sorry, ma'am."

"How'd you end up here?"

"I was a soldier. Got bit. Survived. There are a good number of us here. And here we are. Just go ahead in."

The supervisor's office was the same gray as Corinne's bedroom. Janet glanced up at her, then waved her over. "You'll probably want to see this."

Tara was on the television, looking beautiful and put together in a dark blue suit. "The way that we treat the infected is inexcusable," she said. "My mother is a hero. She served in the war. She was bitten when she tackled a zombie to save a young family. And there are other heroes, locked behind those walls. Is that really how we want to thank them?"

Parental pride mixed with mortification in Corinne's belly. "She's been looking for a cause to champion for years, now."

Janet rubbed her temples. "Is all that true? Did you tackle a zombie to save a baby or some shit?"

Corinne nodded. "That's what happened."

"Damn it. This would be easier if she was making that up. I'm sure she means well. And I know that you didn't do a thing to encourage her, but she has no idea what she's talking about."

Tara was still giving her impassioned speech. "I recently learned of an invention that would allow infected individuals walk among us without fear—an invention that would give them their freedom while keeping everyone safe."

Janet sat back in her chair. "This is the best bit."

"It's called a Life Collar. As long as the infected person is still a human, it's completely safe. But if they turn, the controlled explosives contained in the collar will destroy the living zombie before it can harm anyone."

"A Life Collar?" Corinne asked.

"I've heard stories of them testing the things back east. Reports were… mixed. I know you're new here, and I understand how hard it is to accept that the lives we had before we were bitten are really and truly over, but that girl is going to cause us nothing but trouble. There have always been murmurs in congress about the cost of the infected shelters. Any sort of incident could give them the ammunition they need to shut down the shelters and quietly dispose of all of us."

"Can I ask you something?" Corinne sat down, still staring at the screen.

"Shoot."

"Do they really smell like food?"

Janet grimaced. "Yeah. They do. And we really don't want that tidbit spread around."

"She's not going to let it go, even if I ask her to. She's… very stubborn."

Janet sighed. "Of course she is. Do you know how much pull she has?"

"Well, she's dating the governor."

"Damn it."

"I'm sorry."

"I wish this had taken her longer to put together. I've already received an invitation for you to attend the governor's ball in six weeks. I was hoping that she was lying—hoping we'd have some reason to turn her down. But I don't think we're going to be able to fight this."

Fear fluttered in Corinne's belly. "I don't want to go."

Janet gave her a grim smile. "That's good. Shows that you're sane, that you understand what you'll be going into. But I don't think you're going to have much of a choice."

Corinne imagined Tara hugging her and smelling like food. Then she imagined a bomb collar strapped around her own neck. She shuddered.

"I hate to pile on more bad news, but we also got this in the mail for you." Janet handed her a thick manila envelope.

"What it is?"

The return address was a law office that she'd never heard of. She opened the envelope and scanned the paperwork. "My husband is requesting a divorce. Irreconcilable differences."

"I guessed. We get a lot of those."

Corinne felt numb. She was thankful for that—she didn't want to have an incident now, on top of everything else.

"Is there anything else?"

"Try not to spread the news about the governor's ball around. There are some here who would jump at the chance to get out of here. I'm pretty relieved that you don't seem to be one of them. Go get some rest, and we'll touch base later in the week, once I have more info about your schedule."

Corinne went straight to Nancy's room. When Nancy answered the door, Corinne pushed in and flopped on her hard, narrow bed. The room was almost identical to her own, but much neater.

She threw her arm over her face and moaned.

"That bad, huh?" Nancy said. "What's this?" She pulled the divorce papers out of Corinne's hand and shuffled through them. "Ooof. Cold. I'm so sorry, Corinne."

"That's not even the worst of it," Corinne said, and explained about Tara and the ball and the collar.

"Wait, so he's divorcing you, even though there's a chance that you could get out of here?"

"I don't even know if Tara talked to him about her plans."

"Hmph. I bet the media will have a field day if they hear about it."

"I don't want to go out there," Corinne said.

"Are you kidding? You can't really want to stay locked up here for the rest of your life."

"It's better than the alternative."

"I guess a creepy exploding collar is pretty bad."

"That's bad enough. But what if it malfunctions? And you remember what Danny smelled like. Do you really want to be out in a crowded place, full of normal humans all smelling 'delicious'?"

"I see your point. But we've only been here for a couple of days, and I'm already getting stir crazy. I miss Danny so much it hurts. Ugh, I'm sorry, that was a really terrible thing to say."

"It's not your fault that Darnell hates me."

"I'm sure he doesn't hate you," Nancy said.

Corinne pressed the heels of her hands against her eyes. "I'm pretty sure he does. The divorce papers shouldn't be a surprise—I just wasn't thinking."

"How could he possibly hate you? You said you guys had a good marriage."

"We did. But I'm a zombie now. At least, I am to him."

"What are you going to do?"

"I have no idea."

"Well, maybe it'll be okay. Maybe the smell won't even be noticeable, and the collar will actually be comfortable, and Darnell will change his mind."

Corinne wasn't even sure she wanted Darnell to change his mind. She understood his decision. It was the only logical step forward, really. He deserved to be free to find someone else, to not be tethered to a woman that he'd never be able to touch again.

Had he gone straight to the law office after his visit? She imagined the look on his face. He'd never been one to cling to sentimentality. She scrubbed tears away. She imagined him taking comfort in another woman's arms and felt sick.

"And maybe, they'll find a magic cure for us and the zombie threat will end. And maybe everyone in the world will learn to listen to and respect everyone else, and unicorns will appear on a road made of rainbows and fix all the pain in our hearts," Nancy continued softly.

Corinne laughed. "Right."

"How did you and your husband meet?"

"It was toward the end of the war—I'd just lost my sniper." Beautiful, sweet Aasha, with her long black hair and quick, crooked grin. Their post had been overrun, and Aasha had covered the retreat. She'd had a grenade—Corinne remembered the sound of it, behind her. She hadn't looked back, because she'd promised Aasha that she'd do her best to survive. "A runner isn't much use without a sniper. So I was reassigned to a support role. Darnell worked in the camp kitchen."

"That doesn't sound like a great romance, really."

Corinne shrugged. "My sniper was my great romance, but that doesn't mean that I don't love Darnell."

"I thought that your sniper was a woman?"

"She was."

"Oh."

"I'm sorry—I didn't even think—does that bother you?"

Nancy shook her head. "I'm not like my family. We're friends, I don't care who you get horizontal with. But I'm kicking you out. Go get some sleep. I'll swing by early to use your computer, okay?"

"Yeah."

Nancy hugged her. "You can do this."

Corinne blinked back tears. Nancy was such a sweet girl, and stronger than she knew. And it was good to still have one person she could hug.

• • •

Days slipped by. Corinne rotated through jobs. Her sense of smell improved to the point that she could recognize people by their scents, and she was grateful that other infected people didn't smell like food. She stopped bumping her holster when she walked. Nancy ordered a coffee machine and some strange expensive coffee that had apparently been eaten then pooped out by a monkey.

She spent a shift in Observation Station C, which was manned by a small team, each with their own bank of screens. "How common are incidents?" she asked.

The woman next to her shrugged. "It varies. Generally about one or two a week."

"And how often do people—"

"Turn? It happens. Maybe once a month, if I had to nail it down. But like I said, it varies. We had three months without a single incident once. And a week where five people turned. That was a terrible week."

Corinne sat and watched the monitors. She recognized most of the faces by now. They spent their days just like she did. The cameras watched while they slept, dressed, ate, made love, and used the bathroom.

And Nancy was right—the people watching those cameras weren't there to judge. Her shift passed without an incident, and Corinne was glad to be done with it. But she was also glad that she'd done it—the cameras felt more like friends, now. Eyes that watched over her instead of just watching.

She and Nancy were together in the library, relaxing after their work shifts, comparing the jobs they'd worked so far. Corinne liked library duty best; Nancy was looking forward to being done so she could focus on her medical studies.

Dinner was over, and Corinne had half an hour till her marksmanship class. Just enough time to get through a chapter in her current book.

Then Eric dropped an armful of books that he was shelving and started to shake. He clutched his head in his hands. In an instant, Nancy was on her feet, her pistol calmly drawn. The doors and shutters slid closed. Eliana stood from her typing and drew her pistol, too.

Corinne's fingers were fat and clumsy on the holster snap. "Come on Eric, take a deep breath," she said. "It'll be okay. You can pull through this."

He looked up at her and hissed.

Nancy fired, and his eye exploded. She emptied the rest of her clip into his skull, then took the gun off of his body and emptied it, too. Blood and brain matter splattered onto her clothes and the books all around them.

Corinne stood, frozen, her gun still holstered.

Nancy stared down at the body, her face pale. She closed her eyes and started to shake.

"Oh, no. No, no, no." Corinne ran forward and grabbed Nancy's face. Her cheeks were icy. She remembered Thomas's hands during her first incident, how they'd help pull her back. "Remember yourself, Nancy. Remember Danny. Remember coffee. You can't do this now."

Nancy shuddered, then relaxed into Corinne's arms. A half-hysterical giggle escaped her lips. "Remember coffee." She gave the camera a weak wave and the doors hissed open.

Eliana holstered her gun and glared at Corinne. "That was an idiotic move. It's one thing to freeze up and not be able to even draw your weapon; it's another to interpose yourself in my shot. You got lucky this time, but don't pull that shit again."

A team filed in to clear away Eric's body. Nancy was covered in gore, and some of it had ended up on Corinne, as well.

Corinne wrapped an arm around Nancy's shoulder and ignored Eliana. "Come on, let's go get cleaned up."

"I've never killed anyone before," Nancy said.

"Eric was already gone when you took your shot," Corinne said. "You didn't kill him, the zombie that bit him did. It just took a while."

"Eliana is a huge bitch, but she's right. You took a huge risk, running up to me."

"I'd do it again."

"I'd rather you not have to."

"Well, I guess you'd better start working on a cure, then. You're going to be a hot-shot doctor, right?"

Nancy laughed. "I'll see what I can do."

Corinne saw her to her room. Nancy stopped in the doorway. "Thanks, Corinne. I—you saved me, I'm pretty sure. I was losing it."

Corinne hugged her again, then went to her own to shower and change. Just as she stepped into the water, someone knocked on the door. Panic edged her stomach. She didn't want to deal with news about the governor's ball right now. She wrapped herself in a towel and went to the door.

Thomas stood there, glowering, but he looked surprised when she answered in a towel. "You're late for marksmanship class."

"Nancy shot Eric," Corinne said.

"I heard."

"I was covered in blood."

"I can see that." He reached out and brushed some off her cheek. "But that's no excuse to skip your lesson." He crossed his arms over his chest. "I'll wait."

"Then wait," she snapped. She didn't need his overbearing crap right now. She left the door open and stalked back to the bathroom.

"Corinne."

She paused. "What?"

"I was worried about you."

She sighed. "I'm—I'll be fine. I'll be ready in a few minutes, okay?" She stood in the shower for a few minutes and let the water pound against her skin. She wanted to cry for Eric, but she couldn't. Her eyes were dried out. Her soul felt dried out, too.

She'd lost her family early in the war, long before there was any sign that the humans might win. She'd considered giving up, just walking out into the scrubby wilderness that the zombies ruled and letting them rip her limb from limb. Her blood would be bright red on the sand. If there were enough of them, you didn't get back up.

She'd signed up to be a runner instead. Found new purpose, found new friends. Found Aasha, then Darnell. It started with putting one foot in front of the other, with breathing in and out.

When she got dressed, strapping her holster around her waist felt natural and normal.

"Let's go," she said, walking past Thomas, who'd perched on the edge of her unmade bed.

He followed without a word.

She donned her protective goggles and earmuffs and started shooting.

"You're too stiff," Thomas said.

She pretended not to hear him. She finished her clip. Next time, Nancy might not be there to save her ass. Next time, it might be Nancy.

She blinked back tears. At least her girls were safe. She would never need to shoot one of her daughters in the head.

She reached for a clip to reload, and Thomas pulled the gun from her hands. He loaded it for her and handed it to her. She tried not to look at him. She didn't need to see pity in his eyes.

She thought about his mother, facing her bitten children. Would she have been able to shoot her own infected children? Or would she have taken the same path out that his mother did?

But she already knew the answer to that. The easy way out had never been for her.

Thomas stood behind her and adjusted her stance, tugging her wrist, lowering her elbow. She could feel his breath on her cheek, but couldn't hear it through the earmuffs. He smelled like cordite and ivory soap, and beneath that, like Thomas. His chest pressed against her back.

She fired, and the shot went straight through the target's head.

"Nice. But don't get cocky."

"Shut up."

"I knew you could hear me."

She took a deep breath, aimed, and fired. A second bullet hole appeared next to the first.

"It looks like she can be taught, after all."

Corinne laughed. In spite of all of the horrors of the day, she could still laugh. It was a surprise. "You're actually pretty funny," she said.

"Not enough people know that about me," he said.

"Were you really worried about me?"

"Yeah. I was."

"Eliana told me off for running up to Nancy to bring her back."

"Well, it was a stupid thing to do."

"Was it stupid when you did it for me?"

Thomas gave her a rueful grin. "Yeah. But it was a more calculated risk. Changing in front of an outsider is always dangerous. Like Janet is constantly reminding anyone she talks to, we're very dependent on goodwill from the everyday citizen. There are always people who just want to have us killed. We don't want to remind people that we're monsters."

"I wish I could forget."

"You will. For a minute here and there. And then remembering again will be even worse."

"That's not very comforting."

"It wasn't meant to be. Finish your clip."

She took the rest of her shots. Two just missed the black outline, but the rest hit.

"That's enough for tonight."

Corinne nodded and started cleaning her gun.

"I heard a troubling rumor the other day," Thomas said.

"About what?"

"About you and the Governor's Ball."

Corinne winced.

"So, it's true then?"

"I'm not supposed to talk about it."

"Well, it's hard to keep a secret in here. Is it true that they're calling those idiotic head bombs "Life Collars" now?"

"Yeah."

He rubbed his forehead. "How much did Janet tell you about the things?”

“Not much.”

“Well, on the plus side, I’ve heard that they are very effective.”

“That’s something, at least.”

“I also heard that they don’t make any differentiation between episodes. Even if you’d pull through, the collar won’t know that. And boom.”

“So, I’d better hope not to get too stressed in the huge ballroom with everyone staring at me and all smelling like food.”

“Like prey.”

“What?”

“It’s not like they smell like they rolled around in cinnamon sugar. They smell like prey, and we’re predators.”

“Again, that’s not exactly comforting.”

“Say no.”

“Do you really think they’d let me say no?”

“Put some spin on it—tell them that you just don’t want to risk putting anyone in any danger on your account.”

“Thomas, if Janet could get me out of it, she would have.”

“Well, maybe some good will come of it. You’ll get to see your husband.”

“He’s not my husband anymore.”

“What?”

“He filed for divorce. I mailed the paperwork back this morning.”

“He divorced you?”

“Yes.”

“Even knowing that you might be able to get out?”

“I don’t know what he knew.”

“Well, I’ll tell you something I know. He’s an idiot.”

Corinne rubbed the Z tattoo on her wrist. “He’s always hated zombies. He never wanted to talk about his life before he met me, and I didn’t press. But it was bad.”

“It was bad for everyone.”

“You saw his face after my episode. He thinks of me as a zombie now. He couldn’t stay married to me.”

“Like I said—he’s an idiot. You’re not a zombie.”

“But I could be, at any second.”

"That's true, but it's not all that you are."

"Isn't it? I'm not a wife anymore. And I'm hardly a mother. My daughters will smell like food—like prey. God, that's even worse. Anyway—we're not exactly normal, anymore, are we? Our healing speed is crazy. My sense of smell is even crazier. And I feel better than I have in years. My knees don't ache. I have more energy than I've had in decades. Just because no one talks about these things doesn't make them less true. What are we, exactly, if not monsters?"

"You're still a friend. To Nancy—to me." He stepped close. "I care about you, Corinne. I haven't cared about anyone in a long time—it's too easy to lose people, here. But you—"

"What about me?"

"You actually took the time to see me. No one has done that in a long time. I—I'd started to forget there was a person behind my mask, till you pulled it away"

Corinne touched his cheek. A part of her mind reminded her of the cameras, of the fact that the ink was hardly dry on her divorce papers, of a thousand other reasons that this was a bad idea.

She kissed him anyway.

• • •

They woke to a sharp knock on Thomas's door. "Corinne, you have a visitor."

She kissed Thomas's shoulder. "I hope this is quick—if Nancy hears about us from someone else, she'll be pissed."

He murmured something incomprehensible.

She grinned as she pulled on her wrinkled clothes. She'd imagined him as a morning person.

Devon waited in the hallway. "Do you want to change?" he asked.

"Should I?" Corinne asked. "Who is down there?"

"Your daughter. With a baby. Your granddaughter, I think. It was wearing pink."

That meant it was Kendall, who probably wouldn't notice if Corinne showed up in a potato sack. "It's fine." Walking toward the visitation room was a strange mix of emotions. She was excited to see her daughter and granddaughter, but there was an odd distant feeling, too. Like they weren't really hers anymore.

The guard stopped in the doorway. "I'll be right here if you need anything," he said.

Kendall stood by the glass, with Melody napping on her hip. The baby was, in fact, wearing pink. "Hey, Mom."

"Good morning."

"You look good. Healthy. It's weird to see you wearing a pistol, though."

"We're required to carry them. Just in case." She didn't elaborate, but Kendall just nodded.

"I'm sorry it's taken me so long to get back here."

"I understand. I'm sure you've been busy."

"I—Dad told me about the divorce."

Corinne didn't know what to say to that, so she just nodded. Memories from last night flooded into her mind, and she blushed.

"He just doesn't get it," Kendall said.

"Doesn't get what?"

"That you're a hero. That what you did—you did it for us. For me and Melody. He's so wrapped up in trying to find a way to blame you, to make it easier to let you go. I just—I want you to know that I don't feel that way. That you're still my mother, no matter what." Kendall reached a hand through the tiny window, and Corinne took it. Kendall's palm was clammy and real against her own. But her hand felt fragile, like butterfly wings between her fingers.

"Thank you, sweetie."

Tears shone in Kendall's eyes. "We all miss you. Tara's working on some scheme to get you out of here."

"It's really not so bad in here, I promise."

"Maybe not, but it's still a prison."

"I think it blurs the line between prison and sanctuary. At least I'm safe in here. If I turn—" she remembered Eric, his blood red on her shirt, and shuddered.

"I've heard that people can last years, even decades, before turning. You can't want to stay here for the rest of your life."

Corinne squeezed Kendall's hand gently, then pulled away. She pinched the bridge her nose, and caught the scent of Kendall's sweat on her palm. Her stomach turned. It was one thing to know how normal humans smelled, another to actually experience it. Thomas was right—it wasn't really like food, but it was compelling. And now

35

that she knew it, she could smell it, wafting through the tiny hole in the wall. She could smell Melody, too. She understood now, why the zombies always went for babies first. She pushed the horror away, buried it deep, and forced a smile. "Well, there is a swimming pool."

"Tara was telling me about these collars—"

"No, Kendall. I'm sorry, but it's not what I want. I don't want to live out there, feeling like a freak, wearing a collar that could explode at any second."

"Not even if it meant getting your family back?"

"You don't understand."

"Then help me understand! You love Dad. I know you do. You can't be ready to just let him walk away! You can't really want to not see Melody grow up! You've always been so strong—you taught me to fight for what I want."

"I also taught you to pick your battles."

"Are you saying that we're not worth fighting for?"

"Of course not," Corinne said, stung.

"Then what is it? Do you really believe that you're a monster now?"

"Not right this second. But I could be."

"But the collar would stop you."

If Nancy had been wearing a collar, she would have died last night. If Corinne had been collared, she wouldn't have lasted a single day. She shook her head. There had been a time when she didn't have any secrets from her family—a time when she couldn't imagine lying to Kendall. Was that time really only a month ago? "Do you want Melody to see my head explode? There are reasons that the program wasn't implemented, Kendall."

She comforted herself that it wasn't even really a lie.

Kendall winced. "Of course I don't want her seeing that. But I also want her to know you." Melody woke from her nap and stirred against Kendall's chest. "Sometimes, it feels like you're dead."

Corinne sighed. "Maybe that's for the best."

Kendall shook her head. "I don't believe that. I won't believe it." The baby let out a wail. Kendall pressed her palm to the glass. "Can I do anything for you? Bring you anything? Take a message to Dad?"

Corinne shook her head. Anything that she could ask for— chocolate or orange juice or even some of her books—felt petty and small. "I love you."

"I love you too, Mom."

• • •

Thomas waited outside, across the open doorway from Devon. They both looked worried. "I'm fine," she snapped, harsher than she intended. She wiped the hand that Kendall had held on her jeans, hoping the scent wouldn't linger.

"Janet would like to see you later today. At 8pm." Devon said.

"Okay."

"Come on, let's get some breakfast," Thomas took her hand and pulled her away from the visitation room.

"What if they're right? What if we could live normal lives out there, with the collars? Maybe we could get used to the smell. What if my life isn't over?"

"Your life isn't over, Corinne. It's just different. And there's nothing wrong with accepting that and moving on. You're not betraying anyone."

"But—"

"You said it yourself. We're different. We heal faster, we're stronger and healthier. All of our senses are sharpened. And it all gets stronger, the longer you're infected. And the changes are noticeable. It's not so noticeable, just among ourselves. That's part of why we hide behind these walls. We don't want them to fear us. If they learn to fear us, we are in serious trouble."

"I know that."

"I know you do. And I'm sure your family loves you. But what if they see your changes and start to wonder if you're really still you?"

Corinne laughed. "If what you're saying is true, maybe they'd be right to wonder?"

"They're not, and you know it. You know you're the same person that you were before. The same brave, caring, self-sacrificing person. You're here because you put yourself between a zombie and a family. And yesterday, you put yourself in danger for Nancy. You haven't changed."

"Do you ever wonder what sort of person you'd be if you hadn't been bitten?" Corinne asked. "I mean, you've lived longer infected that you did before."

"I try not to think about it. I take one day at a time, and try to be grateful that I'm alive."

They arrived at the cafeteria, and Corinne pulled Thomas to the table that she and Nancy normally shared.

The younger woman was halfway through her breakfast. "It's about time you got here, I was starting to worry that you were going to skip the most important meal of the day." Nancy glanced up, then did a double take. "Are you two holding hands?"

"Yes," Thomas said.

"So, you're a romantic item now?"

"Yes," Thomas said again.

Corinne was surprised by how happy that made her. She'd imagined skulking in hallways, stealing kisses in the shadows. But then, that would be pointless here.

"Since when?"

"Last night."

"Oh, so that's why you're late."

Corinne sat down and stole a muffin off of Nancy's plate. "Actually, we're late because my daughter came to visit."

"Oh! Any news about the—" Nancy glanced at Thomas. "The thing?"

"No, it was my other daughter."

"Oh."

"I know about the thing," Thomas said.

"Oh," Nancy said.

"I didn't tell him," Corinne said. "The word's out somehow."

"It wasn't me."

"I believe you," Corinne said. "But the word is spreading somehow, and I don't think that's good news."

"I'm going to grab us some food," Thomas said. "You two can stay here and plot. Do you have any requests?"

"The oatmeal is good this morning," Nancy said.

"Oatmeal sounds great." Corinne smiled up at him. "Thanks."

He kissed her cheek and walked away.

"I hate to say I told you so," Nancy said, "But I totally did."

Corinne laughed. "Yeah, I suppose you did."

"And now he's fetching you breakfast and kissing you on the cheek and holding your hand in front of everyone."

"Well, we have some first-hand experience with how hard it is to keep a secret around this place," Corinne said.

"That's true. I wonder who blabbed."

Eliana strode over to their table and glared down her nose at them. "I need a new assistant, after last night. You're it, Corinne. Report to the library as soon as possible."

"I haven't done my full rotation yet."

"Do you not want to be the new library assistant? I'm sure I could request someone else. I just assumed that you'd appreciate the position, since you spend so much time in the library already."

"Wait. You requested me?" Corinne asked, stunned. If she'd been asked to make a list of people who wanted to see less of her, Eliana would have been at the very top of the list.

"Yes. I did."

"Oh. Well, thank you. I'll be there as soon as I can."

"Good. Don't dawdle."

Thomas slid into a chair next to her with his tray. "What did she want?"

Corinne shrugged. "To give me a job."

One of the guards hurried into the room, weaving around tables. He gave Thomas a quick salute, then his eyes locked on Corinne. "Janet needs you in her office."

"I thought our meeting wasn't till 8."

"The plan changed."

"I'll tell Eliana that you were called away," Nancy said.

Thomas pressed an apple into her hand and kissed her. "Eat at least that. And be careful. Count to ten when things get rough. And if all else fails, try punching something."

"Punching something?"

"I'll explain later."

"Okay." The apple's firm flesh crunched and dented under her fingers, and she stifled a shudder at the reminder of her strength. She ate it mechanically and followed the guard. He was a stranger, and she found herself missing Devon.

Janet stood behind her desk, scowling down at a slim briefcase. "The governor is sending a car in ten minutes."

"What? Why?"

Janet shrugged. "They just told me they were coming, and ordered me to get you ready." She opened the latches on the briefcase with a sharp click. "They sent this ahead."

It looked like a simple silver choker, but it was too thick. Corinne picked it up. It was heavy. "It won't be comfortable, will it?"

Janet shook her head. "I'm sorry, Corinne."

Corinne held it to her throat. It closed with a faint click and grew uncomfortably hot against her skin. She tugged at it, and it opened and clattered to the floor.

"Here," the guard said, picking it up. "I can lock it for you, ma'am."

"Can it wait?" Corinne asked.

Janet shook her head. "It's better to get used to it, I think."

Corinne took a deep breath. "Okay."

The guard closed it around her neck. After the click, there was a deep thunk.

"Is it supposed to be hot?" Corinne asked.

"Yes, I think so," Janet said. "It's the sensors."

Corinne sat down. She wanted to rip the thing from her neck and run down the hall. To safety. To Thomas.

She might see Darnell later today.

She felt sick.

Janet's phone dinged. "Great. They sent an itinerary for the day," she said. "Apparently the governor wanted to meet you in person before the ball."

He hadn't been keen on meeting her last Christmas. Tara had been angry for weeks after he'd skipped the family dinner. Corinne made herself look at the screen. It looked like the first part of the day was all hairdressers and makeup artists and dress fittings. Then a dinner with the governor and a few privileged guests. "Is there any way for me to screw this up so that I don't have to do the big shindig that doesn't involve my head exploding?" Corinne asked.

Janet barked a laugh. "I wish I knew. If I understood these people—"

An intercom buzzed. "The car is here."

Corinne concentrated on deep breaths.

"I'll need to take your sidearm," Janet said.

Corinne unstrapped it and handed it to her. Her hands shook. "You'll get this back. Hopefully."

The exit was a three-section airlock. Corinne went through them alone. The last door hissed closed behind her, and she stood in the gray morning. An exterior guard stood a few paces away, clad head-to-toe in black body armor, her pistol drawn. There were two more up on the wall with sniper rifles.

She missed the weight of the gun on her hip. She missed the cameras. She felt naked and alone.

The sanctuary was on an island, so they must have brought the car on a ferry. It was a long, black limo. The door swung open as she approached, and Tara stepped out. Corinne stopped a few paces away.

She could already smell her. And the three men in the car. Two with guns, one without.

How had Thomas stayed sane, fighting alongside them during the war? Corinne counted to ten. She imagined the pool—the cool water and the classical music. Her racing heart slowed.

"Hi, Momma." Tara said.

"Good morning," Corinne said.

Tara took half a step forward and held out her arms. "Don't I get a hug?"

Corinne wanted to say no. She tried to remember the last time she hugged her daughter. Had it really been since Christmas, after the party that the governor had skipped?

She hugged her. She could feel the movement of blood in Tara's neck, could feel how easy it would be to crush her bones.

"I'm sorry this is so last minute, but we had a cancellation at the fundraiser tonight, and I thought it might be nice to get you out once before the ball."

"The dinner tonight is a fundraiser?" Corinne asked.

"Yep. $1000 a plate and no one seems upset that you're replacing the other special guest."

"I'm a special guest?"

"Of course you are," said a male voice from inside the limo. A voice that Corinne recognized. "Why don't you two ladies get in here, and we can chat."

Tara grinned and pulled Corrine into the ridiculous car. "It is about time that you two met."

The governor was about five years younger than Corinne, in good shape for his age, with thick silver-shot black hair and dark eyes. He gave Corinne his best smile. "It's an honor, ma'am. I understand that you're quite the hero."

"There were a lot of heroes during the war," Corinne said. The governor himself had been on the front lines, from what Corrine had heard. He didn't smell afraid, and Corinne found herself respecting that.

"And not quite as many now. I'm so sorry about what happened to you. To have a zombie free in our city—it's intolerable. We're still not sure how it got through the defenses."

Sweat gathered under the hot metal of the collar and dripped down Corinne's neck. The limo somehow felt tiny, the air too close and thick. "Can we open the windows?" Corinne asked.

"No, I'm sorry—we have to keep them up for security reasons. But we can turn the AC up." Tara fiddled with a knob, and cold air blasted Corinne's ankles. It helped a little. Corinne took deep breaths and counted to ten. "So, what is the fundraiser for tonight?"

"We're just raising money for Lee's campaign," Tara said.

Corinne looked out the window. The limo bumped up onto a ramp and then onto a ferry. "Can I go stand on the deck?" she asked.

"Of course! You're free to wander—you're not a prisoner anymore," the governor said.

"The Sanctuary isn't a prison," Corinne said, but she climbed out of the limo. She didn't want to waste time arguing with him that she could spend looking at the water.

The cool ocean air brushed her face, and for the first time, she truly enjoyed her heightened sense of smell.

After a few minutes, Tara joined her at the railing. "I'm sorry to foist you off onto the hair and makeup people, but I have meetings all day. And since everything was so last minute, I wasn't able to coordinate with Daddy and Kendall. At least this way you'll have time to plan what look to showcase at the ball."

Tara was downwind, and that helped, but the collar was hot and heavy and a constant reminder that she didn't belong here. "I don't want to go to the ball, Tara."

"What? Why in the world not?"

Corinne searched for a reason that she could actually share. She shrugged. "I'm just not sure that I'm up to it."

"Daddy will be there."

Corinne stared at the water. "He doesn't want to see me."

"Kendall and I both think he's being ridiculous."

"You didn't live through the war. Your father knows firsthand what I could become, and he wants no part of it. And I can't blame him."

"He's being a bigot."

"That's not fair."

"Your vows were for better or for worse," Tara said. "Would you divorce him if it was the other way around?"

Corinne tried to imagine it. What would Darnell have done if their roles were reversed? "I wouldn't need to divorce him. He would kill himself."

"That's not funny."

"No." They'd had one suicide since Corinne had been in the sanctuary. A man, a little older than Corinne. They'd given him his sidearm, and he'd promptly turned it on himself. Darnell would have done the same thing. She wondered if he was disappointed that she hadn't.

Of course he was. That was why he'd divorced her. She gripped the rail tight, felt the metal strain.

"You're serious. You really think he'd kill himself."

"I do. He might want to kill me, if he has the chance." A thrill of fear surged through Corinne's belly. The collar burned against her throat. He wouldn't be the only one—she didn't doubt that Nancy's family would have killed her if not for Danny.

"He would never hurt you."

"I doubt he sees me as me anymore."

Tara pursed her lips and looked away.

"He's said as much, hasn't he."

"He's just afraid Momma. You're different now, and he's not great at dealing with change. But he'll come around. He's certainly not going to assassinate you."

The political ramifications of an assassination might actually be good for the Sanctuary system. They'd be much better off with a martyr than a monster. She scanned the empty horizon. She'd learned a lot about snipers during the war—she wondered if they could get a headshot to look like the collar exploding.

She wondered if Janet had thought about it.

"Please, Tara. You have to let this crusade—and me—go. I wish things were different, I really do. I would love to come home again and be with your father and just slip back into my life again, but that's not how life works. You can't put the pieces back together. You can't turn the clock back."

"But you can, Momma. With the collar—"

Corinne lifted her chin. "Touch it."

"What?"

"Just do it, Tara."

Her daughter obeyed, then snatched her hand back. "It's hot!"

"Yes."

"Well, I'm sure they can fix that, somehow. It doesn't have to be so uncomfortable."

"Tara—"

"No, Momma. You don't get it. I am not letting this go. I'm not giving you up. I love you, and no matter what Daddy says, you're still my mother. There is nothing that can change that. You can try to be a martyr all you like, you can keep your secrets and think that you're protecting us, you can make that sad, wise face that drives everyone crazy—none of it changes the fact that you are my mother, and I am not letting you go."

"I—"

"You never told us about what happened during the war, but I looked it up. I know all about how you're the last survivor of your hometown, how you teamed up with a sniper who died in action, how you ended up in the camp where Daddy met you. I've seen all of your records. And I don't believe for a second that you would have let any of them go without a fight. You know what it's like to lose people you love. I don't want to lose you. Don't push me away."

Corinne swallowed. "Okay."

"You thought this was just a career ploy, didn't you?"

Corinne sighed. "I suppose I did."

Tara grinned. "Don't get me wrong, it's a great move for my career, and I'm going to take full advantage of your hero status. But that's not my motivation. I'm fighting for you, whether you want me to or not."

"And what if I really don't want you to? What if I think I can be happy in the shelter? What if I don't want to fit back into the broken pieces of my life?"

"You're just mad at Daddy."

"I have a lover."

Tara's eyebrows shot up. "I don't believe you."

"His name is Thomas."

"Well, he can come, too. It serves Daddy right. He's an idiot."

"That's what Thomas said, too."

"Well, maybe I'll like him."

"Tara—"

"I told you, I'm not letting this go."

Corinne sighed. "I know."

• • •

The rest of the day passed slowly. The makeup girl cooed over how young Corinne's skin looked, and she tried not to feel impatient as they dressed her up like a doll. They tested outfits for the ball, then settled on something less dramatic for the dinner. They were all restrictive and uncomfortable. Corinne couldn't bring herself to care.

She tried to imagine how she'd feel in Tara's position. She tried to imagine how she'd feel if their positions were reversed.

But mostly, she just thought about going home. About surviving this day by putting one foot in front of the other, taking deep breaths, counting to ten.

The food at the fundraiser was better than anything she'd had in a long time, but she couldn't enjoy it.

Tara drove her back to the ferry. They didn't talk. Corinne got out of the car without saying goodbye.

Tara rolled her window down. "I'm sorry, Momma. If I was a different person, I might be able to just let you go, let you hide in the sanctuary with your lover. But I can't."

"I understand." Corinne said. A tiny, cold part of her heart thought about how easy it would be to kill this stupid little girl. She wondered if telling Tara that would do a bit of good. She doubted it.

Another black-clad guard escorted her onto the ferry. She enjoyed

45

the wind and moonlight and the sound of the waves.

When she got home, Thomas was waiting for her. He unlatched the collar and held her. "How was it?"

"Not good."

"Janet wants to meet with you tomorrow morning."

"Not now?"

"I asked her to give you the evening off."

"Thanks."

"Let's go to my room."

"Okay." Once the door hissed closed, she flopped onto his bed. "How did you stand it?"

"The fighting helped. Rest times were hard, though."

"How did the fighting help?"

"Remember when you asked me how I've held out so long?"

Corinne nodded.

"I do actually have a theory."

"Tell me."

"Well, what have you heard about how the zombie plague started?"

Corinne frowned. "Well, I thought we didn't know anything, really. It started somewhere in the Middle East, then spread across Europe and Asia before the rest of the world."

"I think it was a failed military enhancement program."

"Why?"

Thomas held out his hands. "Look at us. We're everything an army wants its soldiers to be. Strong, fast, quick-healing. Why would a natural virus give us heightened senses? It had to have been created in a lab. But something went wrong, and the test subjects became monsters. They infected the people they killed, and the virus turned the corpses into soldiers, too. They eat flesh, but they never attack each other. The normal ones would never attack one of us either. Because we're all part of the same army."

"And that theory hasn't been passed around because we don't want people to know about us."

"Exactly."

"So, what does that have to do with controlling it?"

"If we're soldiers, we're meant to fight. I think regular spikes of adrenalin help keep it under control. That's part of why I require that everyone spend at least some time at the shooting range, why we started the hand-to-hand classes. You should start going to those, by the way."

"Why keep this secret?"

"Do you really think that everyone in here could keep their mouths shut? There are some people who do get regular visitors. If the population ever gets an idea of what we really are—I don't think it would be good for us."

"Will you be my teacher?"

"What do you mean?"

"Teach me to fight."

"Of course I'll teach you. You just have to promise me one thing."

"What?"

"When I turn, you have to stop me. I—I can tell it's coming. I think I still have some time. I hope I do. But no one's ever survived as long as I have. I'm afraid of what I'll become. Promise me that you won't let me hurt anyone."

The cold place in Corinne's heart expanded. "What if I'm not there when you turn?"

"Just promise."

"Why not get a collar? They're not comfortable, but it'd be more reliable than me."

Thomas said. "Promise you won't laugh."

"About what?"

"I'm about to say something pretty sappy."

"Oh?"

"I don't want to miss a single moment that I could be spending with you. I've pulled through a lot of incidents. I don't want to know that the next one would be my last. I haven't had someone to care about—someone to share my time with—for a very long time, and I don't want to miss any of it."

Corinne leaned her head on his chest. "What makes me so special? There are lots of other women here."

"Why does anyone fall in love?" Thomas said.

"We've been together for 24 hours," Corinne said.

"I've known since that moment in the hall when you called me on my bullshit. I'm sorry if it's too much, or too fast—"

Corinne shook her head. "It's okay. I love you, too." A tiny voice noted that she'd never been very good at being alone, that she'd always moved fast from one relationship to the next.

She told that voice to shut up, and pulled Thomas close.

• • •

She reported to Janet the next morning.

Janet listed to her full story, scowling. "So, she's not going to stop trying to get you out of here, even though you told her you want to stay?"

Corinne shrugged. "I told you she was stubborn."

Janet rubbed her temples. "Makes me glad I never had kids. No offense."

"None taken."

"Do you have any ideas on how to handle this?"

Corinne shrugged. "I can try appealing to the governor."

"Well, I suppose that's our plan, then. I see that Eliana's requested you in the library."

"Yeah."

"Be careful of her. She's one of the ones who most wants out of here."

"Thanks for the warning. I guess I'd better get to work."

"Go ahead. I'll call you if I need you."

• • •

Eliana glanced at her as she walked in. "There's a pile of shelving that needs done," she said, waving toward an overflowing cart. Corinne grimaced. It didn't look like she'd lifted a finger yesterday.

The bloodstains had vanished from the shelves and carpet, and if any books had been ruined, they'd been cleared out. It looked like nothing had happened. Corinne wondered if there was a single place in the building that hadn't been scrubbed clean of bloodstains.

She finished the shelving and went for a cup of coffee. Eliana followed her into the small room. "I heard they let you out yesterday," she said.

Corinne nodded. Secrets were impossible here—she wasn't sure why she'd even bothered trying.

"Why?"

"My daughter is campaigning for our rights and wants to use me

48

as her poster child."

"Can I do anything to help?"

Corinne had been ready for scathing jealousy or sneering superiority, but Eliana's earnest tone took her completely off guard.

Eliana held up her hands. "Don't get me wrong—I'd clearly be a better example than you are—I'm already famous, and I'm far less threatening than you are. But your daughter is the one with the necessary connections, so I'm willing to play along."

"Aren't you at all worried about having an episode or hurting someone?"

Eliana shrugged. "I'm sure they'll have safety measures in place. And I never have episodes. I want to actually be able to do live readings. I want to sign books and eat in lovely restaurants with grand views and go for walks along the beach. I want a huge private bedroom with no cameras in it. I can't have any of that trapped in here."

"I'll—I'll give it some thought," Corinne said.

"Do that." Eliana poured herself some coffee. "You know where to find me."

• • •

Corinne dragged Nancy down to the gym when their shifts were over. She explained Thomas's theory, careful to keep her voice low. "So, we're going to start sparring," she finished.

"You, me, and Thomas? Doesn't that make me a bit of a third wheel?" Nancy asked.

"You're my best friend—I want to keep you around as long as possible. And you promised me that you'd find a cure, remember? Keeping you alive is a completely valid goal."

Nancy laughed, her eyes bright. "I've never really had a best friend before." She blinked a couple of times. "I'm glad that you still want me around."

"Of course I do!" Corinne said.

"I mean, I'd understand. You've got a new boyfriend and all of the drama with your kids—"

"It sounds like you've had some shitty friends in the past," Corinne said.

Nancy wiped her eyes with the back of one hand. "Yeah, I guess so."

"Well, you don't now. Come on, let's learn how to best punch each other in the face."

• • •

Days fell into a normal pattern. Corinne and Nancy both picked up hand-to-hand fighting incredibly quickly. It felt natural. They also started lifting weights and doing runs on the obstacle course. Corinne had never been able to do a single pull up in her life, and now she could scale vertical walls, then leap from the top and pull herself up onto a higher ledge, before dropping straight down over fifteen feet and sprinting to the end.

Watching Thomas run the course was a pure joy—all of her lovers had been fit, but Corinne had never seen anything as graceful as Thomas at a flat sprint.

Nancy caught her staring and nudged her with a grin. "Shut up," Corinne muttered.

"I didn't say anything. I certainly didn't point out that you were drooling a little, just there."

Corinne blushed. "He's just—"

"I get it."

"What about you? Do you have your eye on any of the men in the compound?"

Nancy shook her head. "Not yet."

"Sorry, I—"

Nancy shook her head again. "It's okay, really. It's good that you've moved on. I wish I could too—I need to. But I guess I have to talk to Danny again, first. And I just don't want to. I can't think of him without remembering how he smelled. Anyway, I'm going to get cleaned up before dinner. I'll meet you in the cafeteria?"

"Yeah, that sounds good."

• • •

Nancy was excited to use Thomas' insight to apply to her medical research. She hoped that the new angle would lead to a breakthrough. Corrine hoped so, too.

Corinne read a lot and managed to avoid giving Eliana a solid answer about her plans.

The day of the Governor's Ball came much too soon.

Thomas walked her to Janet's office. She clicked the collar around her throat, and it was hot in a moment.

"Come back to me," he said.

"I will." She did feel calmer, now. The regular sparring sessions helped.

Tara waited outside, and this time she'd brought Kendall and Melody instead of the Governor.

Corinne took shallow breaths through her mouth and managed a something that she hoped resembled a loving smile. "Good morning."

The girls exchanged a look. "We have a surprise for you," Kendall said.

Corinne smelled him the instant before Tara dragged him out of the car. Her hand went to the sidearm that wasn't there.

Darnell just glared at her.

Her hand dropped to her side, but she shifted into a fighting stance. She didn't smell a gun, and there was no way he could take her without one.

"Mom! What are you doing?" Tara snapped. "Dad's promised to be on his best behavior."

He'd always carried a knife during the war.

Yes, there. Strapped to his left leg. It wouldn't be enough, if he tried something. She looked at the knife, then met his eyes. "Then I guess I should be on my best behavior, too."

"Girls, that thing is not your mother," Darnell snapped. "Surely you can see that, now."

"Dad, you promised!" Kendall hissed. She pulled Melody tight to her chest.

"Why did you come here?" Corinne asked, keeping her eyes trained on Darnell. "It can't really be just because they asked you to."

Darnell shrugged. "I hoped that maybe you'd let your guard down. But I guess you're too clever for that, zombie."

"I've always been clever."

"You haven't always been a monster."

"I'm not a monster now."

"No? Because you're clearly not the woman I married and spent thirty years with."

"You're right. I'm not your wife anymore. But that was your

choice, not mine."

"I bet it didn't take you long to find someone else, though, did it?"

Corinne glared at him. Kendall looked stunned, and Tara looked furious, but both clearly had no idea what to do.

"I've always known that I only landed you because I moved faster than anyone else. I used to think that made me incredibly lucky," Darnell said.

"And what do you think now?"

"That maybe you've always been a bit of a monster—that you'll do whatever you need to in order to survive. That our life only existed because it was the path of least resistance for you."

"I'm not sorry that I didn't kill myself, Darnell."

"I was thinking that maybe I'd do it for you."

"That's not going to happen."

"No? I've always been good with a knife."

"You're not good enough."

"Oh, are they training you in there? Building an army of zombies to take over the country? There are people—"

"Shut up!" Kendall screamed. "Stop it! Stop it, both if you!"

Melody wailed.

Tara pushed them both toward the car. "Neither of you are going to kill the other, okay? We have to get moving—the ferry can't wait forever."

"This is a bad idea," Corinne said. "Maybe I should ride in the front?" There were men with guns in the front, but no Darnell, and no Melody. The baby's scent made her sick.

"Get in," Tara ordered.

Corinne obeyed reluctantly, holding her breath. Darnell followed. He didn't take his eyes off of her as he settled into his seat. Kendall climbed into the car after them, then leaned her forehead against Melody's and cried silently. Tara stared out the window.

"You girls can see that I'm right now, can't you?" Darnell said.

"Shut up, Dad," Tara said.

In another life, Corinne would be the one smoothing everything out. Soothing Darnell's anger, drying Kendall's tears, getting Tara to smile. She got out of the car as soon as it stopped on the ferry and went to the railing. Her family would have to pull itself together without her.

Or not. At the moment, she couldn't bring herself to care.

• • •

"You are different," Tara said, approaching the railing. "It's impossible not to see it."

"Then let me go," Corinne said. "Please."

"No." Tara took a deep breath. "I don't care how much you've changed. Dad's wrong—you're not a monster. You said so yourself. And even if you were, you'd still be my mother. I'd still need you."

"You're a grown woman."

"I'll always need you, Momma."

A few more minutes dragged by. Corinne tried to take comfort in the air and sunshine and water.

Kendall approached, still cradling Melody. "I'm not sure what's happening inside you, Mom," she said. "It's probably not something that I could ever understand. But Dad's the one in the wrong here. He—he told me that he has a knife. Like that would be a comfort."

"I know he has it," Corinne said.

"Well, if either of you is a monster, it's him."

Corinne winced. That didn't seem fair, really. But they'd never understand. It was useless to try to explain.

But the governor was older—he'd been in the war. Maybe she could get him to listen. She clung to that hope as each of her daughters stepped on either side of her and each laid a hand over hers.

• • •

The governor's security guards wouldn't let Darnell keep his knife, so he left. Corinne hoped that she'd never have to see him again.

The day dragged. Corinne, Kendall, and Tara had their hair, nails, and makeup done. They left Melody in day care, which was a relief. She wished the stylists didn't have to be so close to her. Or touch her so often. Eventually, they left.

Kendall left with them, to go check on Melody.

The dress for the ball felt even more restrictive when Tara zipped it up for her. "You really do look great, Momma. Have you been working out?"

"Yeah."

53

"Do you mind waiting here by yourself for a bit? I have some prep work to do."

"That's fine. Do you know if the governor is going to be able to get me the private meeting I requested?"

"I can't make any promises, I think we should be able to make that happen after the ball is over. What do you want to talk to him about?"

"Do you understand what private means?"

"Well, you should know that he's 100% with me about infected's rights."

"I'll keep that in mind."

After she left, Corinne tried going through a tai chi form that Thomas had been teaching her. It was impossible in the stupid dress. The walls felt too close. She counted to ten. She punched the mirror, and her reflection shattered. The cuts on her knuckles healed in minutes.

• • •

A security guard escorted Corinne into the ballroom. She wasn't sure if he was there to protect her from the other guests, the other guests from her, or both. Either way, she wasn't very confident in his abilities. There were too many people, too many scents—each individual human, smelling like prey, but also the perfumes and shampoos and soaps and colognes. The music was too loud, the lights too bright. Her escort led her to a table near the front of the room. She sat down and surveyed the room, desperate to distract herself from the smell. There was a large sunken space in the middle, with tables arranged on each side. Guests entered from the back, and a huge stage dominated the front of the room. There were no good sniper perches, which was a relief.

Corinne spotted four camera crews, twenty armed guards, and another armed man who reeked of barely-contained terror. Her instincts screamed at her to push through the crowd and neutralize him.

She had no way to be sure that he was a possible assassin, no way to know who his target would be, even if he was. The governor wasn't the only high-ranking person in attendance, after all.

But she had a bad feeling.

She half turned to her security guard, about to point her suspect out, but paused. How in the world would she be able to explain her suspicions?

She had to get closer—close enough to stop him if he tried something. She stood. "Am I allowed to dance?"

Her guard looked confused. "I—I don't know, ma'am."

"Well, then I suppose we can safely assume that it's not forbidden. Want to dance?"

His gaze flicked to her wrist. There had been a lot of debate before the stylists decided not to cover her tattoos.

"That's okay, I'll find another partner," Corinne said. She turned and slipped into the crowd.

Corrine had never been good at navigating large groups of people, but it was easier, now. Their movements were easier to anticipate, and her sense of smell helped gauge how close the people outside of her peripheral vision where. Her guard lumbered along behind her, cursing under his breath.

She tapped her target on the shoulder, then hid her hands behind her back. "Would you like to dance?"

Sweat beaded on his forehead, and the smell of his fear was so great that Corinne was could hardly believe that no one else could smell it. "What? No. Get away from me."

"That's not very gentlemanly," Corinne said. "Surely you could spare one dance."

"I said no, lady."

A few of the people around them started glancing their way, and her target's face went red. Corinne leaned in close. "You don't want me to make a scene, do you? Especially not with what you're here for."

His eyes went wide, and he went for the gun. Corinne waited till it was in his hand, then snapped his wrist. She kept the movement small and low—she didn't want the media seeing what she was capable of. The gun clattered to the floor right at her guard's feet as he pushed out of the crowd.

Corinne gasped and stepped back. "This man has a gun!" she shouted.

The crowd fell back, then pressed in. The would-be assassin was quickly on the floor, and Corinne melted back through the crowd to settle into her assigned seat. After the burst of adrenaline, the room didn't feel as hot and close. The collar still chafed.

A few minute later, her guard found her. "How did you do that?" he asked.

"I'm not sure what you mean," Corinne said.

"Did you know about that guy? Did someone tip you off?"

"I just wanted to dance," Corinne said. "We don't do a lot of dancing in the shelter."

He rubbed his temples. "Fine."

"Fine, what?"

He held out his hand. "Let's dance."

• • •

Corinne never got her guard's name, but he turned out to be a decent dancer.

She wondered it Thomas could dance.

Eventually, her guard escorted her to a small room behind the stage. The governor waited inside, gazing down into a tumbler of whisky.

"Thank you for seeing me," Corinne said.

"It's the least I can do." He waved a hand at the guard. "You can go."

"But sir—"

"She's no danger to me, son."

The guard didn't look like he bought that—he didn't seem like an idiot—but he left.

"What did you want to talk to me about?" the governor asked.

"Infected's rights."

"Oh, don't worry. Tara's already bending my ear enough."

Corrine shook her head. "Tara's wrong. You can't just slap a collar around our necks and send us out into the world."

"No? You prefer your prison?"

"It's safest for everyone."

"You don't seem like a threat. And if you turned, the collar would stop you."

"Are you so certain that it's effective?"

He nodded. "I am. I've seen it tested."

"And is that something you really want happening on your streets?"

He frowned at that. "No, I suppose not."

"And these things are not exactly comfortable. You can't really expect people to wear them 24/7."

"Well, they'd be removed for sleep. But from what I understand, people don't usually turn in their sleep."

"What about the minutes before bed? Or after? What if they get up in the middle of the night for a snack, then end up seeking something else to eat instead? It's a bad plan. You were in the war. Tara has no idea how dangerous a living zombie can be. I don't want her to ever have to know."

"If the technology can be improved—"

"Who was that man after?" Corinne asked.

"Me."

"And how did he get that gun past security?"

"We have no idea."

"And there are still no clues on how the zombie that bit me got into the city?"

The governor sighed. "No."

"It seems like you have more important things to worry about. Maybe the issue should just fall off the bottom of your schedule."

"Tara will be furious."

"Find something to distract her with, and she'll get over it. Please. I saved your life tonight—this is what I'm asking in return. Just drop it. Let things stay the way they are."

"I'll see what I can do."

"I want your word."

"I'm a politician."

"Before that, you were a soldier. Promise me that you'll leave the shelters alone, and that you'll drop the life collar initiative."

"Very well. You have my word."

"Thank you, sir."

"Do you have any tips on how to distract your daughter?"

"I hear that planning a wedding can be very involved."

The governor laughed.

"She also loves chocolates."

"That, I knew. Thanks."

"You're welcome, sir. Goodbye. With all due respect, I hope we don't meet again."

• • •

Thomas, Nancy, and Janet were all waiting for her when she got home. She sagged with relief when the doors hissed closed behind her, and again when Thomas took the collar off of her neck.

"We saw the news," Nancy said. "Did you really help to foil assassination attempt?"

"Yeah. I tried to be subtle with it."

"It was well done," Janet said. "Did you get to have a chat with the governor?"

Corinne nodded. "He promised that he'd drop it."

"That's great news. Now we just have to find a way to keep them from summoning you out over and over again," Janet said. "It will probably be even harder now. I'm not sure if your heroic tendencies are good or bad for us."

"I really did try to be subtle," Corinne said.

"Come on, you look exhausted." Thomas took her arm. "That is, if you're done grilling her?"

Janet nodded. "Go on."

• • •

There was a knock on Corinne's door in the early gray hours of the next morning. Thomas muttered something and pulled the pillow over his head. Corinne climbed over him and answered the door.

Devon stood in the hallway, pale and shaking. "Janet turned," he said. "She'd been infected for a long time—more than 10 years, I think. It took a whole squad to put her down. We lost six people."

Corinne glanced at Thomas, who was sitting up, wide awake. "Was she alone when she turned?"

Devon shook his head. "That librarian woman was with her. I—I think she might have turned first. They were arguing. But the gas put her down and she didn't cost us anyone."

"Janet wasn't affected by the gas?" Thomas asked.

"No, sir."

"That's bad. There are quite a few of us who've been here for ten years or longer."

Thomas had been infected for more than three times longer than Janet. Corinne shuddered.

"So, Janet and Eliana are both gone?" Corinne asked.

"Yeah, along with Laura, Steve, Hiro, Alex, Keiko, and Tony."

"And why are you here to tell us this?"

"Because the governor decided to put you in charge."

Corinne needed to sit down. "What?"

"He'd like to talk to you around 10 to discuss the details."

"Right. Okay." Corinne took a deep breath. "I need coffee."

She thought about waking Nancy to use her coffee pot, but headed to the library instead. There was no sense in letting Eliana's coffee go to waste.

Her hands were steady as she measured beans into the grinder and filled the pot with filtered water. "She was so sure that it would be safe for her to leave," Corinne said. "She never had episodes."

Thomas handed her a coffee filter. "We all have episodes. I never saw Eliana at the gym once. She only showed up at the range to scrape through her firearms proficiency tests."

"Maybe she vented through her writing."

"Maybe."

"I didn't like her, but I'm sad that she's gone."

"Me too."

"I did like Janet."

"Me too."

"What am I going to do, Thomas? I can't run this place. I'm a secretary!"

"Janet was a kindergarten teacher. She didn't have any family, but she loved kids. She must have requested to be transferred to Santa Rosa a hundred times over the years."

"Santa Rosa?"

"That's where all they send all the infected kids."

"Oh. See, I don't even know that! How am I supposed to be in charge here?"

"You'll be fine. I think you're a great pick for the job. Plus, your new responsibilities will keep anyone from calling on you to leave."

"Do you think that's why he picked me?"

"I'm pretty certain of it."

"Does it worry you that the gas didn't work?"

"I'm not surprised. But yeah, it's bad news."

"Thomas."

"Hmm?"

"I love you."

"I love you, too."

• • •

They met Nancy for breakfast and caught her up on the news. "Jeeze, your life is a roller coaster," she said.

"Yeah."

"So, other than the heroics, how did yesterday go down?"

Corinne winced. "Darnell showed up with a knife."

"Are you serious? Is he completely insane?"

"I don't know. The girls were pretty shaken by it, I think. I wish he hadn't done it. I don't know if they'll be able to forgive him, and I don't want them losing both of us."

"Well, you can't blame yourself for his crazy. Though I guess it does call your taste into question."

"Hey!" Thomas shot her a glare, and Nancy laughed.

"I'm sure you're a big step up. I know you won't ever go after her with a knife."

A somber silence fell. "No, I wouldn't be using a knife," Thomas said.

"It wouldn't be you," Corinne said. "And it's always possible that I'll turn first."

"Let's talk about something else," Nancy said. "How about the local sports team? Or the weather? Weather's great."

"I am a big fan of weather," Thomas said.

"I wonder if Janet and Eliana were talking about me," Corinne said.

Nancy leaned forward and took her hand. "Even if they were, it wouldn't make it your fault."

"I know. But still, I wonder." Corinne stared at her breakfast. She thought about Tara and Kendall and Darnell and Melody, and how fragile her life here really was.

She knew what she had to do.

• • •

The governor looked tired. Corrine wondered if he'd slept. She settled into Janet's chair and adjusted the laptop screen. "So, I hear you want me to move up in the world."

"It's a solution to both of our problems. Tara can't be mad at me

60

for promoting you, and you'll be too busy to do photo ops at her beck and call."

"And it doesn't matter that there are probably handfuls of more eligible candidates?"

"Not even a little bit."

Corrine didn't want the responsibility of running this place. She wanted to hide in her room with Thomas and refuse to come out. But that wasn't an option.

This was. "Okay. Where do I sign?"

• • •

Corinne's new job involved a lot of paperwork. She managed to get Nancy more funding for her research into a cure and added mandatory fitness training and testing to the firearms proficiency test. She petitioned for coffee machines in the cafeteria and set up a social event schedule.

"It's more like an old folk's home every day," Thomas said, glancing down at her proposed schedule. "Do you really expect people to show up for Bingo?"

"If they don't, we won't schedule it again. Did you know that there are no less than four bands that have been trying to put concerts together for years? Some have had their entire membership turnover since they first filed a request. There's a group of poets trying to get chapbooks printed and distributed. And they want to do monthly poetry readings. There are huge backlogs of social requests here."

"I guess that wasn't Janet's focus."

"She was very security-minded. But I'm trusting that to you."

"You shouldn't depend on me so much."

"Why? Because you're going to die, and it'll probably be soon? By that logic, we shouldn't depend on each other here at all. We should all huddle in our individual rooms and just wait for the end to come. But that's not what we're going to do. We're going to keep going with our heads held high. Maybe Nancy will find a cure. Maybe she won't. Maybe you'll turn tomorrow. Maybe I will. I'm going to live my life as well as I can for as long as I can. And I'm going to help everyone else here do the same."

"I told you that you'd be good at this."

"You're very smart."

"I love you."

"You also have great taste."

"I have an orientation to get to."

She stood and kissed him. "Don't scare them too much. And tell them about Bingo."

"No promises."

"I love you, too."

"I know."

Kendal had sent her a framed copy of their latest family photo to put on her desk. Darnell wasn't in it. But then again, neither was Corinne.

She tried to ignore the ache in her heart.

She went to check in on Nancy and see how the new guard trainees were holding up. On the way, she stopped in the garden and watched a butterfly flit from flower to flower, then flutter up and over the wall.

ABOUT THE AUTHOR

Jamie Lackey lives in Pittsburgh with her husband and cat. Her fiction has appeared in Daily Science *Fiction*, *Beneath Ceaseless Skies*, and the Stoker Award-winning *After Death...* She's a member of the Science Fiction and Fantasy Writers of America. Her short story collection, *One Revolution*, is available on Amazon.com, and her debut novel, *Left Hand Gods*, is forthcoming from Hadley Rille Books. Find her online at www.jamielackey.com.

www.ingramcontent.com/pod-product-compliance
Lightning Source LLC
Chambersburg PA
CBHW070353130626
46556CB00007B/3152